African Animals!

A CHILDREN'S BOOK WITH FACTS AND PICTURES

If you have young children, learning the facts about African Animals is important for the development of your child's imagination. For example, there are many amazing animals found in Africa. You can learn about the biggest, nastiest, fastest, and weirdest creatures.

The information in Facts about the Big 5 is especially valuable for children. Here are some fun facts about these animals for kids. And if you are looking for a fun activity for your next family vacation, take some time to discover all the fascinating facts about these fascinating creatures!

The African hippo is the world's largest living mammal. They cover most of the continent, and their males are territorial and aggressive toward other animals. They can also kill crocodiles.

The Cape Buffalo is also a danger to human life. It kills around 200 people a year. And don't forget about the Thompson's Gazelle, the fastest animal in the world. With its exceptional sense of hearing, sight, and smell, it can run away from predators and even evade attacks.

The giraffe is the largest land animal and the most distinctive among African animals. With a long neck and stilt-like legs, it is the tallest land animal. Its height allows it to eat plants and leaves that are out of reach for other animals.

The Catalogue of Life recognizes eight different species, but some authorities only recognize one. Its horn-like growths on the top of its head give it a distinct personality.

The Nile crocodile is the biggest reptile in Africa, killing hundreds of people each year. The goliath frog is an unusually large animal, measuring over a foot long! There are more than 1,100 species of mammals and over 2,600 species of birds living in Africa.

You can also find a colony of penguins in South Africa. These animals are attracted to cold currents and can walk underwater.

A baby elephant is also called a calf. An African elephant's mother can remain pregnant for 22 months and wait anywhere between two and four years for her next calf. The calf can weigh over 91 kilograms when it is born and can communicate with its mother through its trunk.

The hippopotamus can be dangerous because of its erratic habits. But it can be used to kill humans and other predators.

The baby elephant is called a calf. An elephant calf can weigh up to 91 kilograms. It can communicate with its mother through the mother's trunk. These animals are highly intelligent and have incredible senses.

For example, the hippopotamus is the largest land mammal in the world! And its horns can be seen from the air. Its tusk is capable of reaching great distances.

In Africa, antelopes are the most common animals. They cover the entire continent. They have a stout face, and their ears are shaped like a horn. They also have a distinctively long tail. Several species of hippopotamus can live in the wild.

These are just a few of the most interesting facts about African Animals for kids. These are just a few of the fascinating facts about African animals.

Africa is home to many interesting animals. For example, the Nile crocodile is the largest reptile in Africa and kills hundreds of people every year. In addition to crocodiles, there are goliath frogs, which are up to a foot in length.

Additionally, Africa is home to over 2,600 species of birds and mammals. In addition, there are a number of penguin colonies, and their species is the most widely distributed in Africa.

The hippo is the most common animal in Africa. Its territory covers the continent. The female hippo kills approximately 200 people a year. Moreover, it is the fastest animal in the world. Its ears are so sharp, it can easily avoid predators.

Despite the dangers associated with the hippo, the African apes are a wonderful and diverse place to visit.

9 781071 708613